Grubby's Romance

Story by:
Ken Forsse

Illustrated by:
David High
Russell Hicks
Valerie Edwards
Rennie Rau

WORLDS OF WONDER™

Grubby™ Newton Gimmick™ Princess Aruzia™ Leota™ Wooly What's-It™ Prince Arin™ Fobs™

Page 1

L.B., they're going to do something with that flying boat.

L.B. had pushed the red button on the portable reducing machine.

Oh, I'm going to the annual spring dance.

The dance was being held inside of a hollow tree.

Karen and Grubby spent
a lot of time together the
next few days.

When we got there, Karen was building a kind of shell around herself.

Karen had come out of her cocoon and she was a beautiful butterfly.

The tiny airship took off into a calm sky.

Karen and the other butterflies had to fly off to fill the summer sky with beauty.